WHAT UNCLES DO BEST

BY **Laura Numeroff**

ILLUSTRATED BY

Lynn Munsinger

SIMON & SCHUSTER BOOKS FOR YOUNG READERS
NEW YORK   LONDON   TORONTO   SYDNEY   SINGAPORE

Uncles can take
you on the
roller coaster,

try to win a prize for you,

and buy you cotton candy.

Uncles can play piano with you,

help you make a triple-decker
sandwich for lunch,

and tell you silly jokes.

Uncles can take you for a drive,

go to the mall with you,

and let you pick out new shoes.

Uncles can help you draw,

make puppets with you,

and build a secret clubhouse.

Uncles can let you watch the late show,

send you home with a goody bag,

and invite you back again and again.

But best of all, uncles can give you
lots and lots of love.

But best of all, aunts can give you
lots and lots of love.

and invite you back again and again.

send you home with a goody bag,

Aunts can let you watch the late show,

and build a secret clubhouse.

make puppets with you,

Aunts can help you draw,

and let you pick out new shoes.

go to the mall with you,

Aunts can take you for a drive,

and tell you silly jokes.

help you make a triple-decker
sandwich for lunch,

Aunts can play piano with you,

and buy you cotton candy.

try to win a prize for you,

Aunts can take
you on the
roller coaster,

WHAT AUNTS DO BEST

BY **Laura Numeroff**

ILLUSTRATED BY

Lynn Munsinger

SIMON & SCHUSTER BOOKS FOR YOUNG READERS

NEW YORK   LONDON   TORONTO   SYDNEY   SINGAPORE